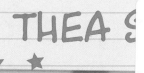

HELLO, I'M THEA!

I'm *Geronimo Stilton*'s sister. As I'm sure you know from my brother's bestselling novels, I'm a special correspondent for *The Rodent's Gazette*, Mouse Island's most famous newspaper. Unlike my 'fraidy mouse brother, I absolutely adore traveling, having adventures, and meeting rodents from all around the world!

The adventure I want to tell you about begins at Mouseford Academy, the school I went to when I was a young mouseling. I had such a great experience there as a student that I came back to teach a journalism class.

When I returned as a grown mouse, I met five really special students: Colette, Nicky, Pamela, Paulina, and Violet. You could hardly imagine five more different mouselings, but they became great friends right away. And they liked me so much that they decided to name their group after me: the Thea Sisters! I was so touched by that, I decided to write about their adventures. So turn the page to read a fabumouse adventure about the

THEA S

Colette

She has a passion for clothing and style, especially anything pink. When she grows up, she wants to be a fashion editor.

Paulina

Cheerful and kind, she loves traveling and meeting rodents from all over the world. She has a magic touch when it comes to technology.

Violet

She's the bookworm of the group, and she loves learning. She enjoys classical music and dreams of becoming a famouse violinist.

THE THEA SISTERS

Nicky

She comes from Australia and is very enthusiastic about sports and nature. She loves being outside and is always ready to get up and go!

Pamela

She is a great mechanic: Give her a screwdriver and she'll fix anything! She loves pizza, which she eats every day, and she loves to cook.

Do you want to help the Thea Sisters in this new adventure? It's not hard — just follow the clues!

When you see this magnifying glass, pay attention: It means there's an important clue on the page. Each time one appears, we'll review the clues so we don't miss anything.

**ARE YOU READY?
A NEW MYSTERY AWAITS!**

Geronimo Stilton

Thea Stilton
AND THE
MADAGASCAR MADNESS

Scholastic Inc.

Copyright © 2015 by Edizioni Piemme S.p.A., Palazzo Mondadori, Via Mondadori 1, 20090 Segrate, Italy. International Rights © Atlantyca S.p.A. English translation © 2016 by Atlantyca S.p.A.

The publisher does not have any control over and does not assume any responsibility for author or third-party websites or their content.

GERONIMO STILTON and THEA STILTON names, characters, and related indicia are copyright, trademark, and exclusive license of Atlantyca S.p.A. All rights reserved. The moral right of the author has been asserted. Based on an original idea by Elisabetta Dami. www.geronimostilton.com

Published by Scholastic Inc., *Publishers since 1920*, 557 Broadway, New York, NY 10012. SCHOLASTIC and associated logos are trademarks and/or registered trademarks of Scholastic Inc.

Stilton is the name of a famous English cheese. It is a registered trademark of the Stilton Cheese Makers' Association. For more information, go to www.stilton-cheese.com.

ISBN 978-1-338-03289-5

Text by Thea Stilton
Original title *Mistero in Madagascar*
Cover by Chiara Balleello (design) and Flavio Ferron (color)
Illustrations by Barbara Pellizzari and Chiara Balleello (design), Valeria Cairoli (color base), and Valentina Grassini (color)
Graphics by Elena Dal Maso

Special thanks to Beth Dunfey
Translated by Emily Clement
Interior design by Becky James

10 9 8 7 6 5 4 3 2   16 17 18 19 20

Printed in the U.S.A.   40
First printing 2016

SUBJECT: ADVENTURE!

The **END** of the school term is always very busy for students, especially the hard-working pupils of Mouseford Academy. But the Thea Sisters — best friends Colette, Nicky, PAm, PAULINA, and **Violet** — had figured out the perfect ReCiPe for spicing up their days of endless studying.

Like any good recipe, this one had a secret ingredient: the MUST DO list! Every time a mouselet took a study break, she'd work on her Must Do list — a list of all the fun things she'd get to do once vacation began.

Which is why, when the THEA SISTERS had finally turned in their last assignments, they rushed back to their rooms. It was time to turn the Must Do list into the **DONE** list!

"We're finally on **Vacation**. Thank goodmouse!" Nicky cried, scurrying into her and Paulina's room. "What are you going to do first?"

"Hmm, let's see . . ." Paulina reflected, taking her LIST out of a drawer. "Well, I could finally read that book about **marine animals** . . . or I could create some new graphics for Colette's blog . . . or I could go to the nursery to buy new **plants** for my patch in the school garden."

"Those all sound like great ideas to me," Nicky agreed, pulling out her own list. "Let's see . . . should I go take a **RUN** around campus, go surfing, or pick out a new sleeping bag for my next camping trip?"

Just then, **two beeps** echoed through the room.

Paulina pulled her phone out of her pocket, and Nicky scurried over to her laptop.

"I just got an email," Nicky said.

"Me too," said Paulina. "It's from Michael and Emma!"

Michael and Emma were two dear friends from the **Green Mice**, an

environmental organization Nicky and Paulina both belonged to. The email's subject line was simply "**ADVENTURE!**"

Curious, the mouselets curled up on Nicky's bed and began reading the long message, which grew more and more interesting with each line.

GREEN MICE

The Green Mice is an organization whose mission is to promote environmental education. The Green Mice organize activities that help students learn about protecting the environment and different animal species.

Michael

Emma

"Dear Nicky and Paulina," the email began. "What do you think about packing up your backpacks and heading to Madagascar?"

Michael and Emma went on to explain that another environmental organization had arranged a WILDERNESS SURVIVAL COMPETITION called ADVENTURE CAMP. It was a program held in the RAIN FOREST of Madagascar, where teams of young environmentalists would be challenged to demonstrate their survival skills — without any outside HELP.

Michael and Emma wanted to participate in the competition — in fact, they were determined to win *first prize*. They wanted to DONATE the prize money to the Green Mice!

There was, however, one obstacle . . .

"We need a team of experienced **GReen MiCe** members to come with us. So we immediately thought of you. You are our most adventurous friends, and from everything we've heard about your buddies Colette, Pam, and Violet, they sound like they'd be **perfect** to join us as well."

For a moment, Nicky and Paulina **LOOKED** at each other. It was so quiet, you could hear a cheese slice drop.

"You know, I think I've figured out what I'm going to do today . . ." Nicky said at last. She was grinning.

Paulina nodded. "I've decided, too . . ."

The mouselets pulled out their Must Do lists and wrote two words across the top:

MADAGASCAR MADNESS!

An Urgent Meeting

Until the day before, Nicky and Paulina would have known just where to find their friends: in the library, studying. But now that exams were finally over, where would their **MUST DO LISTS** have taken them?

"I'm texting the group to meet up at Daisy Bakery," Paulina said, tapping on her phone. "If they're interested in **ADVENTURE CAMP**, we'll need to get ready right away!"

A half hour later . . .

"I'm here, I'm here, I'm here!" trilled Colette, scurrying across the courtyard of Whale Island's most **whisker-licking-good** bakery. She had a brand-new fur-do.

"Why didn't we think of that?" Nicky cried. "Of course the first thing on Coco's Must Do list was getting her **FUR** done at Yvette's!"

A moment later, Violet arrived, her trusty **yoga** mat rolled up under one paw. Pamela trailed after her. She was dressed in a **MECHANIC'S** coveralls, a smile on her snout.

"So, what's up?" asked Pam.

"We've told you about our **friends** Michael and Emma, right?" Nicky began.

Violet nodded. "They were in the **PICTURES** from your most recent Green Mice camping trip."

"We just got an interesting email from them," Paulina said. "And it involves all of us . . ."

As Colette, Pam, and Violet sipped on Swiss cheese smoothies, Nicky and Paulina filled them in. They told their friends all about the **ADVENTURE CAMP** competition in Madagascar and how important it was for the Green Mice to win.

"So we'd have to leave immediately?" asked Colette thoughtfully.

"And spend a week surrounded by nature?" added Pamela.

"And **WILD ANIMALS**?" asked Violet.

Nicky nodded. "Yes. We know it's very last-minute, and we don't expect —"

What's up?

"It would be so *fabumouse* to wake up to the sound of chirping birds," Pam interrupted.

"Just think of all the unique animals and plants we'll **SEE**!" said Violet.

"We need to book our **PLANE TICKETS** right away," said Colette, clapping her paws.

"I'm so *delighted* you like the idea!" cried Paulina. "Although it might mess with your new fur-style, Coco . . ."

"I can stand a week of messy fur if it means I get to go someplace absolutely *amazing*!" Colette laughed. "It'll be an honor."

"**An honor? Really?**" came a squeak from behind Colette.

"Um . . . yes, Ruby," Pamela replied. Mouseford's most *spoiled* student, Ruby Flashyfur, had joined their group. "We're taking off for a place that's —"

"Fabumouse and unique!" interrupted the heiress of the famouse Flashyfur fortune. "I **heard** when I came in. My vacation plans fell through. Perhaps I could **JOIN** you."

"Um, it might not be for you . . ." Violet tried to say.

"It's a **MAGNIFICENT**, exclusive place!" Ruby interrupted, turning **redder** than a cheese rind. "Of course it's for me!"

A magnificent place!

We're going to —

"Well . . . you'll need a sleeping bag," Pamela said. "To sleep in the forest."

"A sleeping bag?"

Ruby asked in **SURPRISE**. "The FOREST? You mean, you're not going to a hotel with a spa?" Her snout grew pale.

"No." Violet smiled. "It's a wilderness survival competition deep in the forests of Madagascar!"

"S-s-survival . . . ?" Ruby stuttered. "Excuse me, but . . . there's something urgent I have to go do!"

"I don't think we'll see her again anytime soon!" Colette laughed as Ruby scampered away faster than the mouse who ran up the clock.

"Too bad," JOKED Pamela. "I would have loved to see the look on her snout when she discovered there aren't any hot tubs or beauty salons in the middle of the forest!"

MADAGASCAR!

- **Continent:**
  Africa
- **Capital:**
  Antananarivo
- **Languages:**
  Malagasy, French
- **Currency:**
  Malagasy ariary

Mozambique

Mozambique
Channel

Indian
Ocean

Antsiranana

Mahajanga

Antananarivo

Antsirabe

Toamasina

Fianarantsoa

Toliara

Madagascar is the fourth-largest island in the world. It's located along the eastern coast of Africa, separated from the African continent by the Mozambique Channel. It is also called the **"Great Red Island"** for the color of its soil, which is rich in iron oxide. Madagascar is known for its unspoiled nature, distinct ecosystems, and unique wildlife. Around 90 percent of all the plant and animal species found in Madagascar are **endemic** — they exist nowhere else on Earth!

MADAGASCAR, HERE WE COME!

Two days later, the Thea Sisters' plane slowly descended. "In ten minutes, we'll touch down in **Madagascar**," the pilot announced.

"Can you believe it?" Paulina said, her snout pressed against the window. "We're really here! And we're going to participate in an *amazing challenge*!"

"We've already completed one big challenge today." Pamela giggled. "Getting Colette on the plane with just a single S U I T C A S E!"

Colette smiled. "As I always say, you don't need to have lots of clothes, just the right clothes."

"I have never heard you say that," Nicky said, thinking of the dozens of suitcases her

friend usually packed.

"You've never heard me say it before, but as of today, it's my **MOTTO**," Colette replied with a wink.

The mouselets landed at the big airport in Antananarivo, Madagascar's capital. They waited a few minutes for another plane that would take them **NORTH** to **ADVENTURE CAMP**.

After their second plane landed, the mouselets collected their luggage and greeted Michael and Emma with a round of hugs.

Outside the airport, they found a **TAXI-BROUSSE**, which would take them to the camp. As they traveled **FARTHER AND FARTHER** away from the city, the five mice found themselves surrounded by ***. PICTURESQUE** countryside.

A **taxi-brousse** (which means "bush taxi" in French) is a common form of transportation in Madagascar. They are buses that connect inhabited areas. Usually, they carry about a dozen passengers.

"Look at all the baobab trees!" cried Violet, admiring the view.

"Some kinds of **baobab** grow only in Madagascar," said Paulina, reading from her MousePhone.

"I do want to hear more about nature," said Pamela, sniffing, "but ever since we left the airport I've been smelling something yummy . . . and I don't think it's the baobabs!"

"Oh, right!" said Emma. "While we were waiting for you, we bought a SNACK."

"Okay, now my

Mofo sakay are spicy fritters made from a flour-and-water dough with pepper, chili peppers, curry, onions, tomatoes, and watercress.

Sambos are fritters similar to a samosa. They are made of filo dough filled with meat, fish, vegetables, or potatoes.

mouth is really **WATERING**!" Pam said. "Why didn't you say so earlier?"

Michael took a sack out of his backpack. "Here, try some. It's *mofo sakay* and *sambos*, and they're still **H◎+**!"

The rodents enjoyed their snack and the view until the *taxi-brousse* stopped.

"We've **arrived**. From here we'll go by paw," Emma announced.

"Before we start hiking, I have to say a few words," Michael said. "I am proud to name Colette, Pam, and Violet honorary members of the **GReen Mice**." He approached them and placed a little **PIN** on each of their jackets. "Without you, we wouldn't be able to participate in what I'm sure is going to be . . .

a FaNTasTiC aDVeNTURE!"

INTRODUCTION TO ADVENTURE

"Okay, mice, we need to head in that _DIRECTION_!" said Nicky, checking the route for camp headquarters.

The **group** made their way through the

C'mon, Coco!

trees and undergrowth. Soon they'd reached the spot on the **MAP** marked with a tent symbol.

There, a rodent with big, dark eyes greeted the Thea Sisters and their friends warmly. "**Welcome!** I am Jonah, the forest ranger responsible for this part of the preserve. I'll be your guide on this **adventure**."

This way!

A group of young rodents stood AROUND Jonah. They were members of the second team participating in Adventure Camp.

Pam stepped forward and introduced herself to one of the **rodents**. "I'm Pam!" Then she noticed that the ratlet couldn't stop scratching his paws. "**ARE YOU OKAY?**"

"Yes — sorry, I don't mean to be rude. It's nice to meet you," said the **young** rat, shaking her paw. "I'm Vinnie . . . and it looks like I'm the favorite dish of the **insects** in this place!"

Are you okay?

Um, I guess so . . .

The ratlet's arms and legs were covered in red bumps.

"Hmm . . . maybe you should change," Pam

suggested. "In a FOREST like this, it's better to cover up as much as you can, so you don't turn into a meal for mosquitoes."

Jonah was squeaking to the other campers. "While we wait for the third and final team, let me tell you a little about the **adventure** we're embarking upon. This forest and the beach nearby will soon be declared a nature preserve . . ."

He explained that the preserve contained a wide variety of animal and plant SPECIES, many of which exist only in Madagascar.

All the rodents participating in

NATURE PRESERVE

A nature preserve is a protected natural area that offers ideal conditions for many different animal and plant species to grow and live safely.

Adventure Camp would learn how to **take care** of the plants and animals there.

"During the next week, you'll be completely immersed in nature," Jonah continued, "and you'll learn to use the resources around you with great care and **RESPECT**. You'll learn to get by **ON YOUR OWN**, without outside help — and without technology."

At those last three **words**, Colette, Pamela, Nicky, and Violet turned to Paulina. She was as still as a statue. You see, Paulina was a huge fan of **technology**. Asking her to survive for days without her MousePhone was like asking a mouse to go without **cheese**!

Paulina swallowed hard. "That . . . that means that . . ."

"Yes, that means that you must paw over every **electronic device** you have with you," Jonah confirmed. He took out a bag and passed it from camper to camper. "You can take only **clothes**, books, and other non-electronic gear along in your backpacks."

Whiskers quivering with worry, Paulina gave up her trusty devices. Jonah SMILED at her. "I know that this is hard now, but trust me: In a few days, you won't even miss them."

You won't miss them!

HERE'S THE
THiRD TEAM!

"**Snout up**, Paulina!" cried Colette, squeezing her friend's paw. "I'll bet Jonah's right. Before you know it, you'll forget all about your **gadgets**."

"I know," her friend squeaked sheepishly. "But for now, every time I see something interesting around us, I put my paw in my **POCKET** to get my phone so I can learn more about it!"

As the **THEA SiSTERS**' team and Vinnie's team explored the clearing, they heard **pawsteps** nearby. Soon a new group of rodents emerged from the forest.

Colette went to **greet** the new arrivals. "**Hi**, I'm Colette!" she said, extending a paw

to the mouselet and ratlet who led the **group**.

The mouselet looked Colette over from toe to tail. "I'm Lisa, and this is my twin brother, Ed."

"I **guess** you're the third team," said Nicky, joining them. "Jonah, the **forest ranger**, just explained what we'd be doing this week."

"Isn't this place the rat's pajamas?" Violet said. "Jonah told us we'll get to take care of the wildlife and learn to survive **ON OUR OWN**."

"But **obviously** we'll need to count on one another, too," Pam said. "We're on different teams, but that doesn't mean that we can't help one another out."

"Oh . . . I **don't** think our team will need your help," Ed replied snootily. "There's really nothing you could teach us about being **explorers**!" He nodded and then headed to the other side of the clearing.

The THEA SISTERS watched him and his team go.

Paulina frowned. "I have a feeling Ed and Lisa DON'T PLAY WELL WITH OTHERS!"

You, help us?!

THE ADVENTURE BEGINS!

Now that the final team had arrived, Jonah declared that the **ADVENTURE CAMP** competition had begun!

"From this moment on, **you must demonstrate** your ability to survive outdoors and your **love** of nature. Only one team will **WIN** the title 'Wilderness Survivors,'" he explained. "Teams will be eliminated one by one, based on how they perform on the challenges. And now the first challenge: build a shelter to rest in **tonight**!"

The young rodents LOOKED around. They had been told not to bring TENTS, and they had expected to find some there. But when they examined their SURROUNDINGS, they realized there was no trace of a tent anywhere!

"I know some of you campers can set up a tent with one paw tied behind your back," said Jonah. At that, Lisa and Ed exchanged smug smiles. "But we don't have any tents here."

The rodents all looked worried.

Everything you need is in these boxes!

"No tents?!" CRIED Vinnie.

Jonah smiled. "This is Adventure Camp — you need to show me you know how to SURVIVE! But don't panic. Everything you'll need is inside these boxes!"

The teams rushed to collect their BOXES and began going through their contents.

"Waterproof fabric and rope . . ." said Emma, taking out the equipment. "How can we use these?"

The Thea Sisters and their friends thought for a moment.

"I remember reading something useful in the GREEN MICE manual," said Paulina at last. "We can find two STRONG trees and tie the rope from one to the other. Then we can drape the sheet of fabric over the rope so it reaches the ground, like a tent."

"**Good idea**," Michael said. "But don't forget, we're in a **rain forest**. So we need to check the ground before we go to sleep to make sure there aren't any **ANIMALS** around."

Pamela nodded. "Of course. And we'll also need to protect the **AREA** where we'll be sleeping from rain."

"Between the equipment that Jonah gave us and what nature has to offer, we have everything we **NEED**," concluded Violet. "Let's get to work! C'mon, move those paws!"

So the Thea Sisters' team began to construct their **TENT**. First they chose two trees. Then they found large branches they could use to clear the **ground** that would become the floor of their shelter.

The rodents covered the area with a thick layer of leaves so they wouldn't have to sleep right on top of the hard, WET ground. Then they placed a sheet of waterproof fabric

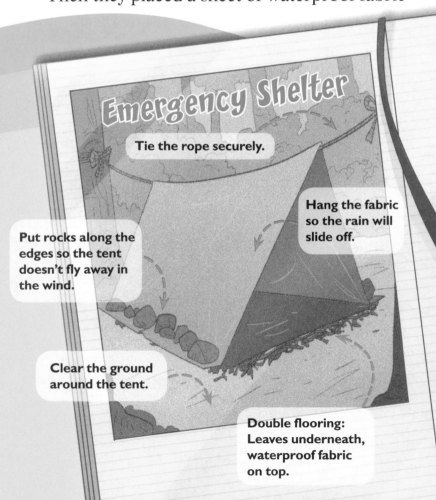

Emergency Shelter

Tie the rope securely.

Hang the fabric so the rain will slide off.

Put rocks along the edges so the tent doesn't fly away in the wind.

Clear the ground around the tent.

Double flooring: Leaves underneath, waterproof fabric on top.

on top. Next they tied a *rope* between the two trees and tossed another large piece of fabric over it. Finally they secured the fabric to the ground with heavy **STONES**.

"What do you think? Looks like a good shelter to me!" Paulina said with **satisfaction**.

Colette studied it for a minute, and then smiled. "It's not a *good* shelter . . .

it's a great shelter!"

A DAY AT THE BEACH!

Evening arrived in a flash. After their long day of hard work, the rodents at Adventure Camp were **sleepier** than Santa Mouse the day after Christmas. They gathered wood for a **FIRE**, chatted for a few minutes, and then retired to their shelters. Most of them fell into a deep **sleep**.

The next morning, Colette was the first one up and about. "Good morning, Vinnie! Did you sleep well?" she called out. But the camper's tired look told her that his answer would be **no**.

Vinnie **shook** his snout, exhausted. "I didn't sleep a wink . . ."

"Me, neither," confessed Lottie, one of his

I didn't sleep a wink...

teammates. "Every time I was about to fall asleep, I heard a CLICK or another strange sound, and the next thing I knew, I was wide awake and terrified!"

"Oh, you poor little scaredy-mice," Lisa said mockingly. "Were you really afraid?"

Paulina glared at Lisa. "If you don't have much experience camping in the wilderness, it's normal to stay awake the first night," she told Lottie.

"Yeah, at night the forest noises can

Huh?!

SNAP!

be **frightening**," Nicky agreed. "But remember, the animals are **MORE AFRAID** of you than you are of them."

I was so afraid!

Just then, Jonah arrived. "Hey, everyone! I hope that you're ready for a new day, because I've got something **SPECIAL** planned. We're going to explore the **coast**!" he said. "But first, let's straighten up camp headquarters."

The Thea Sisters' team and Lisa and Ed's team **got busy** cleaning the campsite and packing up their food and water. Vinnie and Lottie's team was assigned the task of putting out the fire they'd **LIT** that morning.

Once everyone was finished, the group was ready to get going.

The camp was located near the edge of

the forest, and it was only a short **hike** through the brush to a marvemouse beach.

"Can you believe it?" Nicky said, gazing at the horizon. "Sea turtles who live in the Indian Ocean come right here, to this beach in Madagascar, to lay their **eggs**."

Are those pawprints?

Paulina let the **soft** sand pass through her paws. "That's one reason why nature preserves are so important. Many types of **sea turtles** are endangered. But here, their habitat is protected."

Then Paulina suddenly stopped squeaking.

"What's up?" asked Colette, concerned.

"Do those look like pawprints?" she asked, squinting into the distance. "It looks like they're leading into the forest. But we haven't taken that path yet."

Pam shaded her eyes from the sun. "You're right, those look like pawprints. But they're probably from someone in our group who's already GONE THAT WAY."

A few minutes later, the group headed back toward camp headquarters. Everyone was squeaking cheerfully about the amazing sights they'd seen.

But the good spirits from the morning's hike disappeared as they drew closer to the campsite. The air was filled with an odor that COULDN'T BE GOOD . . .

On FiRE!

"Hey, wait a minute," said Emma, stopping suddenly. "Do you smell smoke?"

Paulina sniffed the air. "Yes!" she confirmed, alarmed. "And it's coming from the direction of our camp!"

Faster than a mousetrap spring, the rodents raced through the forest. Once they reached the campsite, they were snout-to-snout with every camper's worst nightmare: a FIRE!

"We've got to put it out before it spreads!" shouted Jonah.

In a panic, Vinnie took off his jacket and tried to stifle the blaze. But he only made things worse. His coat was made of flammable material, and it BURST INTO FLAMES, too!

"Let's run back to the beach and get some water, quick!" Ed ordered his team. They grabbed **POTS** and containers and started running.

"We can't wait for them to get back," Jonah said as Ed's team **DISAPPEARED** into the forest. "Let's gather soil to throw on the flames."

We need water!

"I have an **idea**!" cried Paulina. "Vi, grab your poncho."

Paulina quickly explained her thought — they would look for an area where the ground was **soft**, dig into it with sticks, and then pile dirt onto the spread-out poncho with their **PAWS**.

The rodents put the plan into action. When they'd collected a **pile** of dirt on the poncho, they carried it over and dumped the dirt onto

the flames. **Instantly**,
the fire was put out!

Just then, Ed, Lisa,
and their teammates
RAN out of the
forest, lugging
containers full of water.

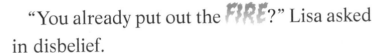

"You already put out the **FIRE**?" Lisa asked
in disbelief.

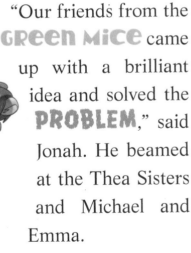

"Our friends from the
GReen MiCe came
up with a brilliant
idea and solved the
PROBLEM," said
Jonah. He beamed
at the Thea Sisters
and Michael and
Emma.

The twins crossed

their paws, **annoyed**.

"Thanks to their quick thinking, we stopped a fire that could have had **GRAVE** consequences," Jonah went on.

"Thanks, Jonah. But I **don't** understand how the fire started in the first place," said Nicky. "We didn't leave the **CAMPFIRE** burning."

Be very careful with fire in the woods! If a fire spreads outside of a designated fire circle, get far away and immediately alert an adult!

Fire grows because of the presence of oxygen. So a fire can be put out by suffocating it — by cutting off its oxygen. Covering a fire with soil or sand will put it out quickly.

Jonah crouched next to the fire pit and **LOOKED THROUGH** it carefully. "No, we didn't leave a big campfire burning, but it wasn't **PUT OUT** correctly." He grabbed a branch and stirred the **embers** left in the campfire. "See? Some of the cinders are still burning. When embers are still live, even the **smallest** gust of wind can catch a **spark** and trigger a fire."

But how . . . ?

The fire started here!

"NICE WORK!"

Ed told Vinnie sarcastically. "You almost let our campground burn dow —"

"Ed, please, it's not your job to scold other campers," Jonah interrupted him. Then he turned to Vinnie and his team. "But it's true: Your TEAM was in charge of putting out the fire, and you didn't do it correctly. You put the forest, its wildlife, and all of us in danger. I must eliminate you from ADVENTURE CAMP."

The Thea Sisters and their friends said good-bye to Vinnie, Lottie, and their teammates, who sadly gathered their things and left.

"I feel bad for them," Colette told her friends. "They weren't very experienced, but they were excited about being here."

"You're sorry for them?" Lisa laughed **SCORNFULLY**. "Don't waste your time on that pack of losers. You should be worrying about your own team, because you're going to be eliminated next!"

You're next!

A SURPRISE ENCOUNTER

The next day, the Green Mice were making their way through the forest when Colette cleared her throat. "Rodents, I don't want you to think that I'm a big meany-mouse or anything, but I'm relieved our team is ON ITS OWN today."

Nicky, Pam, Paulina, Violet, Michael, and Emma smiled. Then Pam said what everyone was thinking. "Don't worry, Coco: We feel EXACTLY the same!"

"I'm sorry to say it," admitted Michael, "but so far the biggest challenge at Adventure Camp is putting up with those snooty rodents!"

After Vinnie and Lottie's team had been

eliminated the day before, the Thea Sisters and their friends had tried to include Ed and Lisa's TEAM in some activities. They'd hoped to get to know the other team **better** by sharing stories and singing songs together.

But Ed and Lisa made it clear they weren't interested. When the Green Mice had invited them to the campfire, they'd retreated to their tent with their TEAMMATES.

Let's go this way!

So that morning, when Jonah had announced that the two **groups** would explore separately, the Green Mice had let out sighs of relief. Each team would look for animals and **NOTE** all the species they found in their logbooks.

"I know that it's a competition and that the GRAND PRIZE is a big deal," said Violet. "But this doesn't have to be such a rat race. Ed and Lisa only seem to care about winning, and that means they miss out on a lot of G**OO**D THINGS!"

Nicky was leading the group, and she

There are broken branches!

stopped suddenly. "Hey, did we already PASS this spot?"

"I don't think so," replied Emma, looking around. "Why?"

"There are some broken BRANCHES," said Nicky, inspecting the plant next to her. "Like someone with a **HEAVY** load passed this way . . ."

"We definitely didn't come this way," Paulina said, frowning.

Her friends drew closer to examine the MYSTERIOUS tracks. Then there was a

CLUES!
WHY ARE THERE BROKEN BRANCHES IN THE FOREST WHEN THE ONLY INHABITANTS OF THE FOREST ARE ANIMALS?

sound from above.

The branches shook, and then a small **ANIMAL** with a red coat leaped down. It was headed right for the rodents!

"It's a lemur!" Michael whispered.

Colette stepped back, worried. "Okay . . . but why does it seem so angry at us?"

The **lemur** is a graceful animal with a long tail and great big eyes. **Lemurs are native exclusively to Madagascar**, and they spend most of their time in trees.

As if in response, a mournful cry came from the bushes behind the rodents.

Moving slowly so as not to frighten the lemur, Paulina inched toward the bush. There was a baby lemur with one paw caught in a snarl of liana vine!

"That must be her baby," whispered Violet. "She's **THREATENING** us because she's afraid we'll hurt it."

Careful not to alarm the **mama** lemur, Nicky bent over the baby. As gently as she could, she freed its trapped 🐾🐾🐾.

Finally free, the little lemur jumped up like a flash and scampered to its mother. Mama and baby snuggled, **happy** to be together again. Then they scrambled up a tree trunk.

Before disappearing into the foliage, the two lemurs stopped a moment and turned to look at the THEA SISTERS and their friends, as if to thank them.

STRANGE PAWSTEPS in THE FOREST

While the Thea Sisters were helping the lemurs, Lisa and Ed's team was *RACING* through the forest. They were hoping to spot lots of different **ANIMALS** — they were determined to show Jonah that they deserved to win this part of the challenge.

Lisa looked up at the top of a tree through a pair of **BiNoCULaRS**. Ed checked the **notepad** with their list of sightings. "Check this out — we've already spotted tons of animals. Geckos, birds,

GECKO

BLUE COUA

SUNSET MOTH

butterflies . . ."

"I bet the **GReen Mice** are stomping around like a pack of pachyderms. They'll scare away all the animals before they even see them!" Lisa giggled.

"Yesterday I chatted a bit with Colette," said Tim, one of the twins' teammates, "and she seems nice to me . . ."

Ed silenced Tim with a glare. "We're here to WIN the contest, not make friends!"

"Ed's right," Lisa barked. "We're here to **beat** the competition, not buddy up with them!"

The rodents continued through the lush forest until they heard the sound of pawsteps in the distance.

"Did you hear that?" asked Ed. "It must be the Green Mice! You were right, Lisa. Their **PaWSTePS** are heavier than our great-uncle Bigbelly's after a seven-course cheese banquet!"

"I've got an idea. **Let's play a trick on them!**" Lisa suggested, grinning spitefully. "Let's hide, and when they walk by, we'll jump out and scare them."

"Great idea," Ed said, chortling.

The twins crept behind a thick **BUSH** and crouched down, trying to stifle their giggles. When the pawsteps grew closer . . .

Let's scare them!

63

"**BOOOOO!**" the twins shouted, jumping out of their hiding spot.

But the smug expressions on their snouts quickly turned into looks of **SURPRISE**. It wasn't their rivals in front of them — it was two grown rodents they'd never seen before.

"**Er . . . e-excuse us**," Ed stuttered.

"Hey, ratto, that wasn't funny," the first unknown rodent snarled.

"We didn't mean to scare you," Lisa tried to explain. "We thought this area was ~~**CLOSED**~~ to the public, so . . ."

"Well, you were wrong," the second rodent spit. "**Don't** mess around in this forest — and **Don't** stick your snouts where they don't belong."

With that, the two rodents **DISAPPEARED** as quickly as they'd appeared.

"**Who do you think they are?**" asked Ed.

He was still shaken from the unexpected run-in. "Should we tell Jonah about them?"

Lisa reflected for a moment, and then **shook** her snout. "No, because then we'll have to **tell him** how we met them, and I don't want him to know we were playing a **prank** on the other team."

"You're right," said Ed. "They're probably just **forest rangers**. I'm sure they're supposed to be here."

CLUES!
THE ONLY PEOPLE AUTHORIZED TO BE IN THIS PART OF THE NATURE PRESERVE ARE ADVENTURE CAMP PARTICIPANTS! SO WHO ARE THE TWO UNKNOWN RODENTS THE TWINS MET?

"Yeah, you're probably right. Let's keep going," said Lisa.

After a few pawsteps, though, she stopped.

"What's this?" she murmured. There was a **gadget peeking** out of a bush close to where they'd first spotted the two unfamiliar rodents.

What's this?!

A STRANGE DISCOVERY

Lisa moved the leaves aside and picked up the object that had drawn her attention. "Check it out. It's a **video camera**!"

"Shhhhhh!" Ed said. "Don't let the rest of the team hear you, or they'll want us to paw it over to Jonah!"

"You're right," **whispered** Lisa. "But do you know what this means? We can film ourselves after all!"

You see, the twins had been very disappointed they'd had to turn in all their **devices**. They were dying to **record** their awesome accomplishments during this adventure. After all, what was the point of having an experience like this if you couldn't take P I C T U R E S to show your friends? But now they could have their cheese and eat it, too!

"Cheese niblets! Let's keep it on the down-low, okay?" Ed said **EAGERLY**. "Maybe we'll even be able to get some good footage to give journalists when they interview us after we W I N the contest."

Ed and Lisa didn't waste a moment. They tiptoed far from the rest of their team, and then turned on the video camera and began FILMING.

But a little while later, when they hit the PLAY button, something strange happened. Half the images

were completely dark, and the other half were in very **bright colors**!

"This footage looks terrible! What went wrong?" cried Lisa, looking at the **display**.

"Maybe the rain forest humidity ruined it," Ed grumbled.

"**BUMMER!** This was going to be the ultimate way to prove our **coolness** to the world," Lisa moaned. She stuffed the **video camera** into her backpack. "Let's take it anyway. Maybe once we're back at camp we can **adjust** it and save what we filmed."

While Ed and Lisa fiddled with their strange camera, the **THEA SISTERS'** team was enjoying their hike back to camp.

"What a day! I can't believe how many animals we spotted," said Paulina, satisfied. "I can't wait to tell Jonah about everything we saw. Maybe we can even suggest some trails for visitors in the future."

"Hey, look at those gorgeous flowers!" cried Pamela, heading for a tree.

"I think they're orchids," said Colette, following her.

But Colette noticed SOMETHING MORE than just flowers. There was a small spider slowly lowering itself into Pamela's thick FUR!

CLUES!
WHO COULD HAVE LEFT THE STRANGE VIDEO CAMERA THAT ED AND LISA FOUND IN THE FOREST?

"Um . . . Pam . . ." said Colette very carefully, knowing how much her friend hated **SPIDERS**. "Those are really beautiful orchids, but maybe . . . maybe you should *MOVE* over a little . . ."

Pam's tail shot straight up like a rocket, and her whiskers quivered.

"What is it?! **CHEESE AND CRACKERS**, is it a spider?!"

"Yes, just a tiny little one," Nicky confirmed. "Really tiny, I promise!"

"Oooooh, I know it's not!"

Check out those flowers!

Um . . . Pam . . .

Pamela said, her squeak shaking. "You're saying it's tiny so I won't lose my cheese, but I'll bet it's an enormouse, gigantic **HAIRY SPIDER** . . ."

Colette reached her paw out to her friend. "Don't worry, it's totally microscopic! But it would be better if you moved anyway, okay?"

Pamela gulped, grabbed her friend's **PAW**, and stretched out a leg to move away. But she accidentally stepped on a DRY BRANCH, and it cracked with a loud *SNAP!*

"**AAAAAHHHHHH!**" Pam shouted in terror. Before her friends could stop her, she scampered off into the forest.

Her teammates looked at one another nervously. Then they scurried after her.

At the end of their dash through the forest, the group of mice found themselves on a beautiful beach.

"**Everything okay?**" asked Nicky, joining her friend.

"Oh, yes," Pamela replied, catching her

I wasn't afraid — I just wanted to go for a swim!

breath. She **blushed** to the roots of her fur. "I wasn't afraid at all . . . I just . . . wanted to bring you here . . . to go for a swim!" she joked.

Everything okay, Pam?

An Unpleasant Surprise

"You know something?" Pamela said as she climbed out of the **WATER**, wringing out her wet fur. "I'm happy that spider crossed our path today, because without it we would have missed this detour to the **beach**."

Her friends agreed. Swimming in these crystal-clear waters was **amazing**!

"This place is truly marvemouse." Violet sighed. "Whether you've got your paws on land or floating in the water, you're always surrounded by wildlife that can't be found **anywhere else in the world**!"

Tired but happy from their **busy** day, the rodents headed back to camp headquarters.

"Hey, we're the **FIRST** ones back," said

Michael. Neither Jonah nor Lisa and Ed's team had returned yet.

"Cool," cried Emma. "I've got an idea — let's light a FIRE and make dinner for everyone."

But when they headed to the tent to put down their things, an **unpleasant surprise** greeted them.

"What happened here?" asked Pamela, running her paw along a **GASH** down one side of their shelter.

"What could have made a tear like that?" asked Colette, puzzled.

Michael slowly shook his snout. "Not 'what' — **WHO.**' That tear is way too CLEAN to have been made by a branch or rock."

"But we're the only ones in the nature preserve. There's no one else around," Emma pointed out.

Just then, a bolt of lightning crossed the sky. Paulina raised her eyes and started to count: "1, 2, 3, 4, 5, 6, 7, 8, 9 . . ."

If you measure the time that passes between lightning and thunder, it's possible to calculate how far off a storm is. The shorter the time between the flash and the thunder, the closer the storm!

BOOOOOOOM!

Thunder rumbled throughout the forest.

"Let's figure out who's responsible later. Right now we have to think about how to repair the damage," said Nicky. "We still have a few minutes, but we'll have to hurry.

The STORM isn't far off!"

The rodents examined the torn fabric, but the longer they GAZED at it, the harder it looked to fix!

"I wish I were a plant right now," Colette said with a sigh. "When it rains, they don't get soaked — the water just slides right off their leaves."

Paulina jumped up. "Way to go, Coco! That's the SOLUTION! Leaves — we need leaves!"

The rodents started looking for fallen fronds and large leaves to place over the damaged wall of the tent.

"I think it's going to WORK," said Nicky. "This way, the rain will hit the SHELTER and then slide right off the leaves!"

"Hey, what's going on?" asked Jonah. He'd just scurried into the campsite along with

Lisa and Ed's team.

Michael quickly filled him in, and Jonah nodded. "**GOOD WORK**. You did the right thing."

The next time lightning **LIT UP** the sky, Paulina didn't have time to count before thunder stopped her.

This will work!

As the first **raindrops** hit the ground, the rodents **SCURRIED** to take cover in their shelters. Little did they know that two pairs of eyes were spying on them from the bushes . . .

CLUES!

HOW DID THE RODENTS' SHELTER GET DAMAGED? AND WHO IS SPYING ON THEIR CAMPSITE?

THIEF!

Paulina had a **restless** night. She tossed and turned like a kitten with a new ball of yarn.

The day that had just ended had been long and full of **adventure**: the hike through the wilderness, the meeting with the **mama** lemur and her sweet baby, the swim in the crystal-clear ocean water, and finally the **SURPRISE** at camp, which had forced the Thea Sisters and their friends to think fast in order to find shelter from the **storm**.

As the rain drummed against the makeshift tent roof and her teammates slept peacefully, Paulina took another look at the big gash.

Michael's words from *earlier* that **afternoon** echoed in her ears: *"Not* *'what' — 'who.' That tear is way too clean to have been made by a branch or rock."*

Was it possible that another rodent had deliberately **sabotaged** their tent? **And if so, who?** Paulina wondered if she and the other Green Mice should be suspicious of Ed and Lisa's team . . .

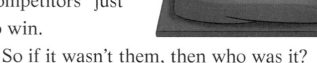

In the dark, Paulina shook her snout. No. She refused to believe it. Lisa and Ed were the most **COMPETITIVE** rodents she'd ever met, but there was no way they'd **sabotage** other competitors just to win.

So if it wasn't them, then who was it?

Paulina was startled from her reverie by **muffled** sounds from outside. Was someone lurking around the **CAMP**? She was about to wake up her friends, but then she thought about how Vinnie and Lottie had worried about the forest's **nighttime** sounds. *"It's just living nature . . ."* Paulina had told them. Comforted by her own good advice, she was at last able to fall asleep.

The next **morning**, when she opened her eyes, sunlight and birdsong greeted her. Paulina grinned. What a great alarm clock!

But that peaceful moment didn't last long . . .

"THIEF! THIEEEEEEF!" shouted a female squeak.

The other campers rushed out of their shelters. They found Lisa in the **middle** of the clearing. She was tearing at her fur.

"Hey, what's going on?" Pamela asked.

"My backpack has disappeared!" Ed explained **ANGRILY**, joining his sister. He was pulling his whiskers in exasperation.

"But . . . that's not possible!" Violet

What happened?

Thieeeeef!

said. "It must be here somewhere. We'll find it!"

The rodents began to search the area surrounding the camp, but with no luck: The backpack had DISAPPEARED like cheddar into a cheese grater.

Paulina thought back to the night before. She was about to tell her friends about the noises she'd heard. As she opened her mouth to squeak, Ed interrupted her thoughts.

It was you!

"I knew you were jealous of our superior survival skills," the ratlet sputtered, GLARING at the Green Mice. "But I didn't think you'd actually resort to stealing our stuff!"

Nicky blinked in confusion. "Wh-what? What do you mean? Are you accusing us?"

"You knew you had no chance of winning fairly, so you tried to **sabotage** us!" Ed said.

"No way! How could you even think that —" Colette began.

But the twins didn't let her finish. They turned tail and MARCHED off.

CLUES!
WHO COULD HAVE
STOLEN ED'S
BACKPACK? AND
WHY? WAS SOMEONE
LURKING AROUND
THE CAMP LAST
NIGHT?

A SHORT TRUCE

The day had gotten off to a dismal start. After **fighting** like cats and rats, the two teams dreaded spending time together. But unfortunately, the day's schedule called for a **group** activity: a trip downriver in a canoe.

When it was time to leave camp, the Adventure Camp contestants were quiet as mice. They walked side by side, their **EYES** on the ground.

But as the rodents paddled through an incredible forest of mangroves, they found peace in their surroundings. They put aside their differences and began chattering like chipmunks.

Even Ed and Lisa seemed content to enjoy

the countryside and the company they were keeping. For the FiRST time since the beginning of this adventure, the twins forgot all about the competition.

As they hiked back to camp, everyone was in a good mood. They nattered happily about the sights they'd seen.

Mangroves are tropical plants that grow along the coast, often at the mouths of rivers. Many have **roots that grow in the water**, becoming visible only at low tide.

"Everything's back to normal now, thank goodmouse," observed Emma as she and Paulina approached the campsite. "Maybe tonight we can play games around the campfire."

Paulina was about to reply when something caught her attention. "What's this scrap here?" she asked, reaching for a piece of paper outside the **supply tent**.

As she drew closer, she realized the campground was a huge mess. The supply tent had been totally trashed! There were **smashed** food packages, cans tossed onto the ground, and **SHARDS** of broken dishes everywhere.

"Oh no! Mouselets, you've got to come see

CLUES!

WHAT IS THE PIECE OF CRUMPLED PAPER DOING IN THE MIDDLE OF THE FOREST? WHO COULD HAVE LEFT IT?

this!" she said, stuffing the scrap of paper into her **POCKET**.

"Do you think **ANIMALS** got into the tent somehow?" Colette asked.

Nicky shook her snout. "I don't think so . . . They left all the packages of food."

"Here we go again," said Ed, **COMING**

What a cat-astrophe!

Look over there!

UP from behind the mouselets.

"What do you mean?" Pamela asked.

"It was our turn to organize the supplies. And this cat-astrophe will make us look bad!" Lisa replied, joining them.

"Are you suggesting we made this mess just to show you up?" Violet asked in disbelief.

Lisa nodded. "First the BACKPACK, now the supplies. You rodents are totally cutthroat! You'll do anything to win!"

"Well maybe it was you mice who sabotaged our tent!" Michael cried.

As the paw-pointing continued, the THEA SISTERS exchanged a look of dismay. Someone wanted to turn the ADVENTURE CAMP teams against each other . . . and it was WORKING!

LISA'S SECRET

"This competition isn't going at all like I *thought* it would . . ." Colette sighed.

"I've had it up to my whiskers with those twins," said Nicky, shaking her snout.

"**I know**," Paulina said, stacking the damaged cans. "Lisa and Ed have great outdoors skills, but it's obvious they've NEVER worked in a team. And that's totally key on an **adventure** like this!"

You see, the GREEN MICE had always taught its members that it was important to treat others kindly. It made for happier days in the field, and it also helped build trust in dangerous situations!

After accusing the Green Mice team of sabotage, Ed and Lisa had scurried away, leaving the Green Mice to **clean up** the mess.

"Look, Lisa must have lost her BANDANNA when she stomped off," said Colette, picking it up.

"Here, give it to me," said Paulina, taking it. "I'll go leave it next to her backpack."

Paulina headed over to Ed and Lisa's tent. She tied the bandanna to one of the BUCKLES on Lisa's pack.

But when PAULINA turned to go, she caught her 🐾🐾🐾 on a backpack strap. She stumbled, grabbing onto a TREE to stop herself from falling.

She was okay, but she'd accidentally dragged Lisa's backpack along with her. It opened, and all its contents spilled out.

"What's this?" cried Paulina, picking up

the **video camera** Lisa had found in the forest.

Paulina shook her snout. Everyone knew there were no **technological** devices allowed in Adventure Camp! At first, she was upset, but then a thought struck her. *Maybe this rule-breaking could prove useful!*

"If Lisa took footage of the camp, then

Oops!

there could be some clues that'll help us figure out who's responsible for all the sabotage," Paulina murmured.

She sat down next to a fallen tree and started to look at what Lisa had **FILMED**. Seeing those strange colors confused her at first, but then she remembered she'd seen images like this before.

Paulina scratched her snout. **"OF COURSE!"** she cried suddenly. "There were images like this in *Creatures of the Night!*"

Let's take a look . . .

Creatures of the Night was the latest **FILM** by James Mouseron, the Thea Sisters' favorite documentary filmmaker.

Nicky and Paulina had gone to **SEE** it a few months earlier, and they'd been impressed by scenes showing the life of **NOCTURNAL** forest animals.

To take this footage, Mouseron had used a **thermal camera** — that is, a special camera that showed images in the dark created by the **HEAT** from animals' bodies. The result was very similar to the video on Lisa's device!

"But why was Lisa using a thermal camera?" Paulina wondered.

It was time to share her strange discovery

with her friends. But when she scrambled to her paws, Paulina realized that she had company. Lisa was right behind her, and judging by the expression on her snout, she wasn't happy.

CLUES!
A THERMAL CAMERA? WHO COULD HAVE LEFT THAT IN THE FOREST? AND WHAT WERE THEY DOING WITH IT?

An Impossible Argument

"**What are you doing?!**" Lisa thundered. She was more furious than a fly stuck in fondue.

Paulina blushed. "I . . . It's not what it looks like! I can **explain**!"

How dare you!

"How dare you go through my things?" demanded Lisa.

The other rodents heard Lisa's angry **squeak** and **realized** something was going on.

"Um, everything okay?" asked Pam.

Lisa silenced her with a **LOOK**. "No, everything is NOT okay. Your little friend here **opened** my backpack and went through my things!"

"Lisa, please, listen to me," pleaded Paulina, mortified. "I didn't mean to snoop, I swear it on a stack of cheese slices! I was just —".

"You were just getting ready for another trick, right?" Ed interrupted her.

That rubbed Emma's fur the wrong way. "Not that old song again. How many times do we have to tell you that we didn't do anything!"

"The facts squeak for themselves," Ed replied scornfully.

"You've been afraid of us since day one, and you'll stoop lower than slugs to beat us!" Lisa added. She snatched back the thermal camera. "Give me that camera! I'm the one who found it!"

Those words shook Paulina. Lisa had said "camera," not "thermal camera," so she

didn't know what it really was! And then she said she'd found it . . .

"Wait a minute, Lisa," Paulina cried. "What do you know about that device? And where did you find it?"

But Lisa was too angry to listen. "From this moment on I'm not saying a single word to you. And the same goes for my team!"

With that, she STORMED OFF. Ed and the rest of the team trailed after her.

"I wasn't snooping in her things," Paulina said, her squeak shaking. "You believe me, right?"

"Of course we believe you!" Nicky cried. "We know you wouldn't do that! Now tell us everything, and we'll figure out what to do together."

SURPRISE CLUE!

Paulina told her friends what had happened: After tying Lisa's BANDANNA to her backpack, she'd tripped and accidentally dumped out all the pack's contents.

"And that's when you found the video camera?" Colette asked.

"Actually, it's not a video camera! I tried to explain, but Lisa didn't let me squeak. I SAW some of the footage. It's a thermal camera," Paulina revealed.

"A thermal camera?" asked Emma, surprised. "Like the ones used to identify people and animals in the DARK?"

Pamela stroked her whiskers thoughtfully. "Why would Lisa have a thermal camera?"

"I don't think it was hers," Paulina

explained. "Her story had more holes than a slice of Swiss! You heard her: First she called it a '**video camera**,' and then she said that she found it in the forest."

"How could she have **found** it in the forest?" Violet asked.

Paulina shook her snout. "I don't know . . ."

"Mouselets, this whole thing smells fishier

Something's not right!

than day-old tuna," Michael DeCLaReD.

Nicky agreed. "I'm starting to think we're **not the only ones** in this forest."

"But that can't be!" Violet objected. "Jonah said this whole area is ~~CLOSED~~ until the grand opening of the nature preserve."

1. The gash in the tent was too clean to have been an accident.

2. Why would an animal carry off an entire backpack?

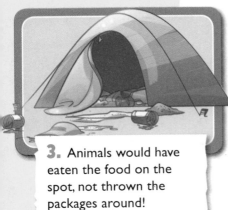

3. Animals would have eaten the food on the spot, not thrown the packages around!

"That's true, but I don't think it's tourists we're dealing with," Nicky said.

"Good point, Nicky," Emma agreed. "No toURISt would bring a thermal camera to record their MeMORIes."

"And the accidents at camp definitely weren't caused by ANIMALS," Colette put in.

PAMELA seemed convinced. "No. But maybe someone wanted us to believe it was animals to SCARE us away . . ."

"That's possible, but who? **And why?**" asked Colette, twisting her tail with worry.

"I don't know," Paulina whispered, digging her paws into her pockets. A moment later, she pulled out a crumpled piece of paper.

"What's that?" asked Violet.

"Just a scrap of paper, I think . . ." Paulina replied, opening up the paper to **SEE** what was on it. "I found it next to the messed-up supplies, and I guess I put it in my pocket." Her squeak trailed off as she examined the scrap.

"Everything okay, Paulina?"

asked Colette, watching her friend **CURIOUSLY**.

A wide smile spread across Paulina's snout, but her eyes didn't leave the paper. "More than okay. I think our *mysterious* visitors left us a clue!"

LET'S REVIEW THE CLUES:
- ED AND LISA ENCOUNTERED TWO STRANGE RODENTS.
- LISA FOUND A THERMAL CAMERA.
- STRANGE ACCIDENTS HAVE HAPPENED AT THE CAMPSITE.

FINDING THE COORDINATES

The mice gathered around Paulina and examined the **crumpled paper**. - - - -

"What is it, a receipt?" Colette asked, looking at the strange **NUMBERS**.

Paulina shook her snout. "No . . . see that little circle next to those numbers? It **indicates** the degrees of an angle. So these aren't just numbers, but . . ."

"**Geographical coordinates!**" Nicky exclaimed.

"Huh?" asked Colette.

"Geographical coordinates are pairs of numbers that indicate a

precise location," Violet explained.

The Green Mice pondered this unexpected clue. Had the sneaky saboteurs dropped this paper?

"So how do we **find** the place marked on this paper?" Violet asked.

"If only I had my MousePhone," Paulina grumbled. "I have a GPS app that would be perfect. You just type in the coordinates, and it instantly shows you the **location** on a map. Plus the best **route** to reach that spot!"

"WELL, actually, you don't need

> Any point in the world can be located using its geographical coordinates of LONGITUDE and LATITUDE.

an app for that," Michael said. "During my first year in the **GReen MiCe**, I took a class in cartography, and I learned how to find **LOCatiONS** using geographical coordinates. I have everything I need — it'll just take a few minutes."

Michael **worked** on the map with a compass and protractor. A few minutes later, he put down his **instruments**. "The location indicated on the paper isn't far from here!" he announced, *POINTING* to a spot on the map.

The mouselets were excited. They were sure they'd find **answers** to their questions in that spot.

"Let's **GO** check it out right away," Paulina

said. "Someone keeps sabotaging our camp, and if the *suspects* are really out there in the forest, we've got to stop them before they put **ADVENTURE CAMP** in any further danger!"

So the Green Mice team headed into the forest.

"Hey, aren't we CLOSE to where we met the mama lemur and her baby?" asked Colette a few minutes later.

"You're right," Paulina said. "We came across them just past that waterfall. This also explains the broken BRANCHES we noticed — they must have been the work of the mysterious intruders!"

"That means we're definitely following the right strand of string cheese," Pam said.

"Here we are!" Michael said, hurrying ahead. He stopped between two tall TREES. "The coordinates are leading us to the SPOT just between these . . ."

Michael trailed off. Once they reached him, the THEA SISTERS and Emma were struck squeakless, too.

Before them lay a full campsite crowded with WOODEN CRATES!

A TRAFFICKERS' HIDEOUT!

"I'd say it's official: We're not **alone** in this forest," said Pamela, stepping into the clearing.

The THEA SiSTERS and their friends explored the camp. Judging by the hammocks **TIED** to the trees, two rodents were staying there . . . two rodents who were very different from the participants in the ADVENTURE CAMP.

"I wonder if Jonah knows there are other campers in this forest," Colette said.

"I'm afraid that these rodents aren't just **campers**," said Michael, dumping out the contents of a bag he'd found under a TREE.

"Hey, those are thermal cameras!" Pam *exclaimed*.

"And not just that," said Emma, emptying another bag. "Flashlights and sticks with loops on the ends!"

"And over here, there are NETS and

There's more over here!

TRAPS!" Nicky added, checking the contents of a large crate.

Violet STARED at the supplies, confused. "What is all this stuff for?"

Paulina found the COURAGE to say what all the Green Mice had guessed by now. "They're for capturing wild ANIMALS!"

"So we're dealing with animal traffickers?!" asked Colette, alarmed.

Paulina nodded. "I read an article about it in the Green Mice newsletter a while back. Animal trafficking is a big problem in Madagascar — and in many other protected places in the world, too."

"Rodents take these unique animals from their natural habitats to sell them to the highest bidder," Nicky added.

"That explains the thermal camera. They used it to identify and locate **nocturnal** animals!" said Pamela.

"And the FLASHLIGHTS and sticks with loops are for flushing out and capturing snakes!" added Paulina.

"After the traffickers **CAPTURE** the animals, they lock them up in these crates, ready to be shipped off . . ." Michael concluded, gesturing around the clearing.

The Thea Sisters and their friends soon realized that one of the crates was **CLOSED**.

They approached it cautiously. Pam grabbed a **screwdriver** and used it to lift the lid and pry out the nails sealing it.

Inside were geckos and chameleons!

FRIGHTENED by the sudden sunlight, the creatures stayed motionless for a moment.

Then they started to scamper up and out of the crate. Soon they'd disappeared into the forest.

"We can't waste any time," said Nicky. "We need to **ALERT** Jonah and the other forest rangers right away!"

"**SHHH! QUiet!**" Emma whispered, looking around. "Someone's coming!"

Tails twitching, the mice turned toward the **BUSHES** they'd passed through earlier.

They heard **pawsteps** coming closer. Then the bushes moved, and when the fronds Parted . . .

"Ed, Lisa, what are you doing here?!"

Colette **cried** in surprise.

Lisa shot her rivals a challenging look. "Simple — we **FOLLOWED** you here. And now we've caught you red-pawed! So, you want to tell us what's going on here?"

"No need, sister dear," Ed sneered. "**I'll**

explain it all for you! This is their hideout, where they plan their **sabotaging** and hide what they steal. Look, my **backpack** is over there!"

"What a load of rotten cheese!" Emma cried.

"You've got the **WRONG** end of the cheese stick, Ed!" Paulina sputtered angrily.

Well . . . we . . .

"Okay, okay, let's keep calm and scurry on," said Colette. "Ed, Lisa, listen to us: We've got **BIGGER** problems than the competition . . ."

The Thea Sisters and their **friends** quickly filled the twins in. They told them about the clue they'd found next to the supply tent, about how it had led them here, and about the thermal cameras and their suspicions.

"For a while now, we've had a feeling someone else was in the forest," Emma finished. "But we couldn't prove it until today!"

Ed and Lisa both had strange expressions on their snouts . . . almost as if they were embarrassed!

"What's up, Ed? Lisa?" Violet asked.

"Well, to tell you the truth . . ." Ed muttered, "a few days ago, we RAN INTO two strange mice . . ."

"And that's when we found the video — um, thermal camera," added Lisa.

Michael's snout dropped open like a hungry cat at feeding time. "But why didn't you tell anyone?"

"Because we wanted to keep the video camera," Ed **SNAPPED**. "And we didn't want you to take advantage of the situation to get ahead!"

"But we wouldn't have done that!" Colette protested.

"Oh, sure," said Lisa. "You never miss a chance to show off! You would've found a way to take it from us and —"

"WELL, WELL, WELL," came a squeak from behind them. "Looks like we have visitors, Fred!"

Caught by **SURPRISE**, the young rodents whirled around. They found themselves snout-to-snout with the two strangers Ed and Lisa had run into a few days before.

It was the animal traffickers!

AN UNPLEASANT ENCOUNTER

"Ah, yes, just a few unexpected guests, Stan," joked Fred. He took a few steps toward the Thea Sisters and their friends. An EVIL grin spread across his snout. "To what do we owe the honor of this visit?"

The young mice SHRANK BACK with fear, but at last Paulina found the courage to squeak.

"We know who you are!" she said. "We know that you're traffickers!"

"Fred, I told you we should STEER CLEAR of these meddling ratlets," Stan muttered, stroking his whiskers. "These snoops are more CURIOUS than tomcats. They keep sticking their silly little snouts into our business!"

"I know, but I had to get my thermal camera back. And then it was such fun watching them wrack their little brains when they found something fishy," Fred replied. He started talking in a high-pitched squeak, in obvious mockery of the campers. "'Who took my backpack?' 'Who sabotaged our TENT?' 'Who moved my cheese?'"

Stan laughed and laughed.

Nicky was boiling like a pot of forgotten fondue. "Do you realize the animals you're trapping are very rare species? Some of them only live in Madagascar. Taking them from their natural environment could mean condemning them to EXTINCTION!"

Fred and Stan didn't seem too interested in Nicky's opinions on the subject. They'd spotted the crate that had held the geckos and chameleons.

"Why is that CRATE open?" Fred barked.

"It's empty!" Michael shouted. "We **freed** the animals you captured!"

"Watch yourself, young rat!" Stan growled, approaching Michael THREATENINGLY.

"Don't waste your time on him," Fred said. "If we hurry, we can get the animals back!"

"Never!" Emma shouted. "We'll report you and have you arrested!"

"I don't think so," Stan sneered, taking some rope out of his bag. "Because you're not GOING anywhere!"

In a flash, the pair had tied the young mice to two big TREES.

"First we'll recapture the animals, and then we'll deal with you," Fred promised. Then he DISAPPEARED into the forest with his partner.

ONE TINY ANT

When they started investigating the **mysterious** events around the camp, the Thea Sisters never imagined they'd end up in a situation like this. They figured they'd be dealing with illegal campers, not animal **traffickers**!

The same went for Ed and Lisa: They had followed their rivals hoping only to catch them **red-pawed**. They were sure they'd seal their victory at Adventure Camp, but instead they were **TIED** to trees next to their rivals!

"This is all your fault!" Lisa burst out. "Why did you come snooping around **HERE**, anyway?"

"Why?" Paulina asked, **annoyed**. "Well,

maybe we wanted to find the true culprits behind all the sabotage you've **_accused_** us of!"

"And actually," said Emma, "if you hadn't followed us, we would have left earlier, and now we'd be at camp calling for **HELP**!"

Violet agreed. "Exactly! But now we're trapped here with you two, and instead of worrying about how we're going to **save** our fur, you're still determined to uncover some kind of **conspiracy** in the competition!"

"Well, if you —" Ed started to reply.

"OKAY, THAT'S ENOUGH!" Paulina

It's all your fault!

Yeah!

cried. "Everyone shut your snouts for a minute, and listen up. We've got to find a way to get out of these ropes before Fred and Stan get back."

"Good plan, Paulina," said Colette. "It'll be **DARK** soon, and then it'll be much harder for us."

"Maybe our TEAMMATES have already realized Lisa and I are missing. They could be looking for us," Ed guessed.

Lisa sighed. "Or maybe they're enjoying a little peace and quiet without us there to **boss** them around . . ."

"Don't beat yourself up," Colette consoled her. "There's always **Jonah**. He's probably looking for us."

"Maybe, but we can't count on the others. We need to take care of **ourselves**!" said Michael, trying to wiggle out of the ropes.

But he quickly realized their bindings were too tight to budge. Michael LOOKED down, discouraged. "What am I saying? We'll never do this on our own!"

Silence fell over the CLEARING. Each rodent was lost in his or her own thoughts.

The mouselets and ratlets were gloomier than a groundhog who's just seen his shadow. Despair was getting the better of them . . . until something caught Nicky's eye.

The piece of bread is too big for just one ant, but it won't give up! It just needs to remember . . .

Not far from her paws, she noticed an **ant** trying to carry off a large piece of BREAD.

The traffickers must have dropped the bread on the ground, but it was too **Heavy** for the ant, who abandoned it and scurried off.

Nicky followed the creature with her eyes, convinced it was *going* to find a different piece of food. Instead she saw the **ant** communicate something to another ant

THERE'S STRENGTH IN NUMBERS!

with a touch of its antennae. That ant did the same to another, and so on.

The little group of ants made their way back to the bread. Together, they easily carried it off toward their anthill.

Nicky smiled. One ant couldn't do much, but a group of ants could do a lot when they worked together.

"You're wrong, Michael!" she said confidently. "We're not alone . . . we're together.

AND TOGETHER WE CAN DO IT!"

WORKING TOGETHER!

As she watched the ants work together, Nicky found inspiration. She was sure her idea would SOLVE their problem!

"There's no way any of us can get free if we each just try on our own," she explained. "But if we work all together, at the same time, maybe we can do it!"

Nicky's plan was very simple: On her count, the mice would try to LIFT their paws up high. That way, they might be able to scoot the rope tied at their elbows up to their shoulders.

"That's a great idea, Nicky," Colette cried. "Once the rope is up to our shoulders and reaches our necks, we can wriggle free!"

And so, the mice began to lift their paws up as one. It seemed impossible, but working together, little by little, they managed to free their bodies from the rope!

Once they were on their paws, untying the knots around their wrists was easy.

The minute they were free, the Thea Sisters and their fellow ADVENTURE CAMPERS scurried through the forest. They REACHED camp just before nightfall.

"Thank goodmouse!" cried Jonah. "I've been worried sick about you. Where have you been?" He looked the young rodents over from paw to tail. Their fur was slick with sweat, and they were covered with dirt.

"Sorry, Jonah. We shouldn't have gone off without telling you where we were headed," said Paulina. "But we made a SERIOUS

C'mon, let's haul tail!

discovery, and we need your help!"

Jonah listened **carefully** to their story. His expression went from worry to shock to grim determination.

"I'm proud of you young mice. You were very BRAVE," he said when they'd finished. "But you've done enough. Now it's time to call in reinforcements!"

With that, Jonah headed toward a wooden CRATE on the edge of the campsite. It had sat unopened since day one.

Let's call for help!

"So, uh, reinforcements are inside that BOX?" Pam asked.

Jonah smiled. "Kind of! Inside are signal flares we can use to call my forest ranger COLLEAGUES. I won't let the animals you freed fall into the paws of those traffickers!"

UNEXPECTED NEWS

Once the signal flares were lit, the THEA SISTERS and their friends waited anxiously for the forest rangers to arrive.

"Let's hope that those two sewer rats haven't **CAPTURED** any more poor, defenseless animals," Nicky said fiercely.

Luckily, it took less than half an hour for Jonah's colleagues to reach the Adventure Camp site.

The young campers sprang to their PAWS and led the forest rangers through the forest. Now that they knew the route, it didn't take long to scurry over to the traffickers' camp. They surprised Fred and Stan as they were trying to ESCAPE with their gear!

That **evening**, all the rodents got together around the campfire to celebrate the arrest of the two traffickers. All the bad feeling between the two teams was cheese under the wheel after everything they'd been through.

The young mice sang campfire songs, told stories, played games, and laughed and laughed.

When they woke up the next morning, though, the campers received some unexpected news . . .

Right after breakfast, Jonah gathered everyone in the center of the campsite.

"First of all, let me say how proud I am of all of you," he said. "Unfortunately, I just heard from the organizers of our ADVENTURE CAMP, and it seems we have a problem . . ."

"What's wrong?" asked Colette, worried.

"The discovery of the animal TRAFFICKERS has upset our plans," Jonah explained. "I'm afraid we have to END the competition before we can declare a winner."

"But that's not fair!" Lisa moaned. "We

worked so hard!"

Jonah sighed. "I know, and I'm sorry. But the **decision** has already been made."

The Thea Sisters and their friends were **silent** for a moment.

"But . . . can we **STAY HERE** anyway?" Nicky asked timidly.

"Of course!" Jonah assured her. "You can stay here as planned, right up till the GRAND OPENING of the nature preserve."

"Okay, then no more long snouts, mouselings!" Paulina said. "We're staying put. And now we can relax and enjoy visiting this *fabumouse place!*"

HOORAY FOR THE PRESERVE!

The Thea Sisters and their friends spent the next few days exploring the forest and beaches all around them. They were determined to enjoy every moment of their time in Madagascar.

On the last day of their trip, the mouselets FOLLOWED Jonah on a breathtaking hike across a long bridge suspended over a ROCKY canyon. It was one of the most fabumouse experiences of their trip.

The day of the grand opening finally came. Many visitors arrived, eager to tour the newly protected AREA. Mr. Leon, the president of the association that had organized Adventure Camp, was there, too.

"Before **opening** the nature preserve, I must say one more thing," said Mr. Leon at the end of his **speech**. "Today we are celebrating this **marvemouse** place and the animals that live here. We owe our thanks to a group of exceptional young mice for helping keep this place pristine: the participants of **ADVENTURE CAMP**! Let's give them a round of applause!"

Give them a paw!

"He's talking about us!" cried Violet, blushing **redder** than a cheese rind. Mr. Leon motioned for the Green Mice and Ed and Lisa to join him on the **podium**.

"These mice have **completed** their assignments with great courage. And now, **thanks to them**, the species that live in this area are safe," Mr. Leon continued. "I

am very proud to tell you that the competition's GRAND PRIZE will be awarded to **BOTH TEAMS**!"

The Thea Sisters and their friends jumped up and down like baby mouselings in a cheese shop. But their celebration was cut short when Lisa squeaked up.

"Mr. Leon, my team and I thank you for this honor," she said. "But we think awarding the prize to both teams isn't right at all!"

It's not right at all!

So Long, Madagascar!

The Thea Sisters and their friends **STARED** at Lisa. The mouselet had become a true friend to them over the last few days. Was she about to turn tail on them now?

Lisa simply smiled at them. Then she cleared her throat and continued.

"It's true that both teams were together when we **alerted** Jonah to the presence of animal traffickers. But it was all thanks to our **RIVAL TEAM** that those two poachers were exposed, and it's only thanks to them that we managed to **escape**! That's why my teammates and I have decided to turn down the prize. **THERE'S ONLY ONE WINNING TEAM HERE, AND IT'S NOT OURS!**"

The Thea Sisters were *moved*. They went to **hug** the mice who only a few days earlier had been their **bitter** rivals.

"We . . . we don't know what to say," Colette said.

"Thanks to you, the **GReen Mice** will finally be able to afford the equipment they've been **dreaming** of for years!" said Emma.

Ed smiled. "You don't need to thank us. You earned it! And as for us . . . well, we already have our **PRiZE**. Just being here in the rain forest, surrounded by this gorgeous **nature**

Thanks!

and such good friends — it's all the thanks we need!"

Once the awards ceremony was over, Colette, Nicky, Pam, Paulina, and Violet packed up their things. It was time to catch their **TAXI-BROUSSE** back to the airport.

But before they left this place full of lush nature and rare animals, the Thea Sisters stopped for a MOMENT to take in the amazing sights that had surrounded them for the past week.

"So long, Madagascar, hope to see you again soon!" Colette said.

Just then, Nicky noticed something out of the corner of her EYE.

"Hey," she whispered, "don't everyone look at once, but someone in the tree to our left has come to say good-bye . . ."

When she saw the mama LEMUR and

her baby, Paulina instinctively put her paw in her pocket, looking for the **MOUSEPHONE** she'd just gotten back.

"Do you want to take a picture?" Violet asked.

"I thought about it for a second," Paulina smiled, removing her empty paw from her pocket. "But I changed my mind. No digital **PHOTO** could be as beautiful as the picture

IN MY MEMORY!"

The Thea Sisters laughed, and smiled at the lemurs. They would never forget the experiences they'd had at **ADVENTURE CAMP**!

Don't miss any of these exciting Thea Sisters adventures!

Thea Stilton and the Dragon's Code

Thea Stilton and the Mountain of Fire

Thea Stilton and the Ghost of the Shipwreck

Thea Stilton and the Secret City

Thea Stilton and the Mystery in Paris

Thea Stilton and the Cherry Blossom Adventure

Thea Stilton and the Star Castaways

Thea Stilton: Big Trouble in the Big Apple

Thea Stilton and the Ice Treasure

Thea Stilton and the Secret of the Old Castle

Thea Stilton and the Blue Scarab Hunt

Thea Stilton and the Prince's Emerald

Thea Stilton and the Mystery on the Orient Express

Thea Stilton and the Dancing Shadows

Thea Stilton and the Legend of the Fire Flowers

Thea Stilton and the Spanish Dance Mission

Thea Stilton and the Journey to the Lion's Den

**Thea Stilton and the
Great Tulip Heist**

**Thea Stilton and the
Chocolate Sabotage**

**Thea Stilton and the
Missing Myth**

**Thea Stilton and the
Lost Letters**

**Thea Stilton and the
Tropical Treasure**

**Thea Stilton and the
Hollywood Hoax**

**Thea Stilton and the
Madagascar Madness**

**Thea Stilton and the
Frozen Fiasco**

And check out my magical special editions!

**THEA STILTON:
THE JOURNEY
TO ATLANTIS**

**THEA STILTON:
THE SECRET OF
THE FAIRIES**

**THEA STILTON:
THE SECRET OF
THE SNOW**

**THEA STILTON:
THE CLOUD
CASTLE**

**THEA STILTON:
THE TREASURE
OF THE SEA**

Be sure to read all my fabumouse adventures!

#1 Lost Treasure of the Emerald Eye

#2 The Curse of the Cheese Pyramid

#3 Cat and Mouse in a Haunted House

#4 I'm Too Fond of My Fur!

#5 Four Mice Deep in the Jungle

#6 Paws Off, Cheddarface!

#7 Red Pizzas for a Blue Count

#8 Attack of the Bandit Cats

#9 A Fabumouse Vacation for Geronimo

#10 All Because of a Cup of Coffee

#11 It's Halloween, You 'Fraidy Mouse!

#12 Merry Christmas, Geronimo!

#13 The Phantom of the Subway

#14 The Temple of the Ruby of Fire

#15 The Mona Mousa Code

#16 A Cheese-Colored Camper

#17 Watch Your Whiskers, Stilton!

#18 Shipwreck on the Pirate Islands

#19 My Name Is Stilton, Geronimo Stilton

#20 Surf's Up, Geronimo!

#21 The Wild, Wild West

#22 The Secret of Cacklefur Castle

A Christmas Tale

#23 Valentine's Day
Disaster

#24 Field Trip to
Niagara Falls

#25 The Search for
Sunken Treasure

#26 The Mummy
with No Name

#27 The Christmas
Toy Factory

#28 Wedding
Crasher

#29 Down and Out
Down Under

#30 The Mouse Island
Marathon

#31 The Mysterious
Cheese Thief

Christmas Catastrophe

#32 Valley of the
Giant Skeletons

#33 Geronimo and the
Gold Medal Mystery

#34 Geronimo Stilton,
Secret Agent

#35 A Very Merry
Christmas

#36 Geronimo's
Valentine

#37 The Race Across
America

#38 A Fabumouse
School Adventure

#39 Singing Sensation

#40 The Karate Mouse

#41 Mighty Mount
Kilimanjaro

#42 The Peculiar
Pumpkin Thief

#43 I'm Not a
Supermouse!

#44 The Giant
Diamond Robbery

#45 Save the White
Whale!

#46 The Haunted
Castle

#47 Run for the Hills, Geronimo!

#48 The Mystery in Venice

#49 The Way of the Samurai

#50 This Hotel Is Haunted!

#51 The Enormouse Pearl Heist

#52 Mouse in Space!

#53 Rumble in the Jungle

#54 Get into Gear, Stilton!

#55 The Golden Statue Plot

#56 Flight of the Red Bandit

The Hunt for the Golden Book

#57 The Stinky Cheese Vacation

#58 The Super Chef Contest

#59 Welcome to Moldy Manor

The Hunt for the Curious Cheese

#60 The Treasure of Easter Island

#61 Mouse House Hunter

#62 Mouse Overboard!

The Hunt for the Secret Papyrus

#63 The Cheese Experiment

#64 Magical Mission

#65 Bollywood Burglary

The Hunt for the Hundredth Key

Don't miss any of my special edition adventures!

THE KINGDOM OF FANTASY

THE QUEST FOR PARADISE:
THE RETURN TO THE KINGDOM OF FANTASY

THE AMAZING VOYAGE:
THE THIRD ADVENTURE IN THE KINGDOM OF FANTASY

THE DRAGON PROPHECY:
THE FOURTH ADVENTURE IN THE KINGDOM OF FANTASY

THE VOLCANO OF FIRE:
THE FIFTH ADVENTURE IN THE KINGDOM OF FANTASY

THE SEARCH FOR TREASURE:
THE SIXTH ADVENTURE IN THE KINGDOM OF FANTASY

THE ENCHANTED CHARMS:
THE SEVENTH ADVENTURE IN THE KINGDOM OF FANTASY

THE PHOENIX OF DESTINY:
AN EPIC KINGDOM OF FANTASY ADVENTURE

THE HOUR OF MAGIC:
THE EIGHTH ADVENTURE IN THE KINGDOM OF FANTASY

THE WIZARD'S WAND:
THE NINTH ADVENTUR IN THE KINGDOM OF FANTASY

THE JOURNEY THROUGH TIME

BACK IN TIME:
THE SECOND JOURNEY THROUGH TIME

THE RACE AGAINST TIME:
THE THIRD JOURNEY THROUGH TIME

LOST IN TIME:
THE FOURTH JOURNEY THROUGH TIME

Meet
CREEPELLA VON CACKLEFUR

I, *Geronimo Stilton*, have a lot of mouse friends, but none as **spooky** as my friend CREEPELLA VON CACKLEFUR! She is an enchanting and MYSTERIOUS mouse with a pet bat named **Bitewing**. YIKES! I'm a real 'fraidy mouse, but even I think CREEPELLA and her family are AWFULLY fascinating. I can't wait for you to read all about CREEPELLA in these a-mouse-ly funny and **spectacularly spooky** tales!

#1 The Thirteen Ghosts

#2 Meet Me in Horrorwood

#3 Ghost Pirate Treasure

#4 Return of the Vampire

#5 Fright Night

#6 Ride for Your Life!

#7 A Suitcase Full of Ghosts

#8 The Phantom of the Theater

THANKS FOR READING,
AND GOOD-BYE UNTIL OUR
NEXT ADVENTURE!